After-School Activities
Are Great

By Debbie Croft

Illustrations by Tamsin Ainslie

On Monday morning, Ms Brett stood at the front
of the school hall and spoke to everyone.

"Boys and girls, we are ready to start our school **assembly**.

Today, Tess, Joshua and André would like
to tell you about the **activities** they do after school.

When they have finished, you can think about
which activity you may like to try."

Tess came forward to speak first.

"Good morning, everyone. My name is Tess.
I would like to tell you why I think playing tennis
is a great after-school activity.

First, playing tennis is a good way to keep fit.
I get lots of exercise when I run around on the tennis court.
Running and stretching for the ball help to make
the muscles in my arms and legs stronger.

Second, playing tennis after school allows me
to meet other children who don't go to our school.
This means I have lots more friends.

On the weekends, I spend time with my friends from school
and my friends from tennis.

Last of all, I enjoy being outside in the fresh air.
I know this helps me to stay healthy.

During the winter, I play tennis on days
when the weather is fine.
I play tennis in the summer, too,
although sometimes I get very hot!

I believe that playing tennis is one of the best
after-school activities."

After Tess had finished her talk, it was Joshua's turn.

"Hello, my name is Joshua.
I believe that my after-school activity is great.
I have an art lesson with Ms Tauranga every Wednesday.

First, I think art is a very good way to show people
the things that are important to me.
I like to make **collage** pictures of plants and animals.
I use different materials, such as paint, crayons,
wool and recycled card.

Second, I like bright colours.
I believe that red and yellow make people feel happy.
Blue can make people feel **calm**.

Last week, I painted a picture of some children at a fair.
Two clowns were giving them balloons.
The bright colours made the painting look very exciting!

Last, I enjoy art because I learn something new every week.
One thing I have learnt is how to make
different **shades** of colour.
Some are lighter and others are darker.

Another thing Ms Tauranga showed me
is how to make cars and buildings in my pictures
look like they are in the distance.
I know that I have to draw the things that are in the distance
smaller than the parts of the picture that are much closer.

I think going to art lessons is the best activity
to do after school."

When Joshua had finished, André got up to speak.

"Hi, my name is André.
Every Monday after school, I go to a lesson
with some other children, where we learn a different language.
Mr Romano is teaching us to speak, read and write Italian.

My friend Carlo is Italian.
He speaks that language at home, with his family.
I want to learn to speak Italian, too.
Carlo and I would like to travel to Italy
when we are older, to visit his **nonna** and **nonno**.

Also, language lessons are fun
because I meet other people who do not go to our school.

We talk about the games we play
and the places we visit on the weekends.
We often laugh because we don't know how
to say some words in Italian!
Mr Romano writes the words we need to learn on a board
to help us remember them.

bianco

rosa

rosso

Last of all, Dad says learning a new language
helps my brain to get exercise.
My brain gets a little more exercise every day
when I try to remember new words in another language.

I really enjoy going to Italian lessons after school."

Papà

Then, Ms Brett spoke to everyone again.

"Thank you, Tess, Joshua and André.
It has been very interesting
to hear about your tennis, art and language lessons.

I'm sure some other children
will want to join in these activities, too.
Next week, we will have a different group of children
sharing why they think their after-school activities
are the best."

Glossary

activities *(noun)*   things that people do, such as sports and hobbies

assembly *(noun)*   a gathering of students and teachers

calm *(adjective)*   quiet and peaceful

collage *(noun)*   artwork made with lots of different materials

nonna and
nonno *(nouns)*   names for Italian grandparents

shades *(noun)*   lighter and darker forms of a colour